You are
Beautifully
&
Wonderfully
Made
Tiger the Mule

Tiger the Mule

WRITTEN BY J. ALLAN SMITH

ILLUSTRATED BY D. W. SMITH

TIGER THE MULE

WRITTEN BY J. ALLAN SMITH

ILLUSTRATED BY D. W. SMITH

HILLIARD PRESS

Tiger the Mule
Copyright 2018 by J. Allan Smith
ISBN 978-0-9990090-5-5

Written by J. Allan Smith
Illustrated by D. W. Smith
Book Design by Miguel Camilo

Published by
Hilliard Press
a division of
The Hilliard Institute for Educational Wellness

Franklin, Tennessee
Oxford, England
Abbeyleix, Ireland
www.hilliardinstitute.com

Dedication

*To my wife, Vicky, the launch pad
for all my elusive dreams.*

6

PART ONE

One cold, wet, windy day in the rolling green pastures of Tennessee, a baby mule was born. His mama was a beautiful Tennessee Walking Horse, and she admired her baby mule and loved him very much. She fed him, protected him, and kept him close to her side everywhere she went.

The owner of the beautiful horse named her baby mule "Tiger" because his coat was orange with black stripes and white socks on his legs. Tiger grew strong and steady under the watchful eyes of his mother.

The owner also watched Tiger grow, and decided to take Tiger from his mother to sell him for a profit.

So when Tiger was only six months old, he was sold and taken to a new farm far from home and away from his mother.

When Tiger got to the new farm, the farm animals only stared at him, and no one wanted to be friends. Tiger felt lonely and scared.

One day, the farm dogs began barking and nipping at Tiger. When the dogs sensed he was scared, one of the dogs bit Tiger's leg. The bite hurt, so Tiger protected himself from the dogs in the only way he knew how—he kicked. Not knowing his new owner was behind him, Tiger accidentally kicked his new owner, who fell to the ground.

The new owner sprang up with an angry huff, grabbed a big stick, and began hitting Tiger. Tiger was confused. Tiger had only kicked to protect himself, like all mules do. He did not mean to hurt his owner. Yet the owner hurt him with the big stick until Tiger was in terrible pain.

Tiger did his best to be a good mule, but there were still times he would get in trouble on the farm. Vegetables were Tiger's favorite food, and there was a tempting vegetable garden near the pasture. Sometimes Tiger would jump the fence, pull up carrots and turnip greens, and have a delicious meal. Each time Tiger jumped the fence, though, his owner would cruelly punish him, leaving poor Tiger in terrible pain. Yet sometimes Tiger would smell the delicious vegetables and jump the fence, only to be beaten again.

12

One day, the owner, who was usually mean and cruel, offered Tiger a slice of an apple. Tiger was so excited by this show of kindness! When he saw the apple in the owner's hand, Tiger opened his mouth wide and took a big bite. In his excitement, Tiger bit his owner's finger. Though it was simply an accident, the owner still punished Tiger, leaving the mule in tremendous pain.

All of the beatings, and the isolation of having no friends on the farm, made Tiger feel lonely and sad.

One day, the unkind owner came out to the pasture, tying a lasso around Tiger's neck and placing a halter on his face. Tiger had worn a halter only once before—when he was taken to the new farm. So Tiger figured he'd be making a trip to a new home. Tiger felt happy because he would be away from the beatings, cruelty, and loneliness.

PART TWO

Tiger's owner sold him to a man named Mr. Smith. Mr. Smith gently led Tiger to a new, green pasture, but Tiger did not want to go to this unfamiliar place. Tiger began kicking and bucking to resist. While he was bucking, Tiger knocked Mr. Smith to the ground.

Then Tiger got very afraid and bucked some more, because he knew he was in for a cruel beating. However, Mr. Smith did not beat Tiger. Instead, Mr. Smith got up, dusted himself off, and whispered kindly to Tiger, "It's all right, boy. I'm not going to hurt you."

Even though Mr. Smith's words sounded soft and kind, because he had no memory of kind treatment from a human, Tiger was distrustful of Mr. Smith.

Every day, Mr. Smith would come to the pasture and visit with Tiger, bringing a block of crispy hay and a bucket of delicious oats. Because he didn't trust Mr. Smith, Tiger was reluctant to let his owner get too close, so Mr. Smith would place the hay and oats on the ground.

Each day, though, Mr. Smith would move the hay and oats a little closer to Tiger.

One day, Mr. Smith held the bucket of oats in his hands instead of putting it on the ground. Tiger could smell the yummy oats and feel his hungry tummy growl. Very slowly, Tiger moved closer, extending his head out toward the oats as far as it would go. When he got close enough to the oats, Tiger threw his head at Mr. Smith, knocking him to the ground. Quickly, Tiger grabbed a mouthful of oats and ran away.

When he looked back toward Mr. Smith, Tiger could see him getting up from the ground and dusting himself off. Tiger could also see the oats that remained in the bucket. He was still awfully hungry, so he turned around to see if Mr. Smith would offer him some more oats.

Mr. Smith was a patient man and did indeed offer Tiger more oats. As slowly as before, Tiger inched toward the bucket. The smell of the oats was irresistible. When Tiger was close enough, Mr. Smith gently touched him on the neck.

Tiger didn't like the feeling of a human touching him because he remembered all the beatings from the past, so he backed away. Still, Tiger was hungry, and he realized that unless he allowed Mr. Smith to touch him, he was not going to get any oats.

Tiger felt afraid, yet tried to be courageous. Slowly, he stepped closer to the bucket of oats, never taking his eyes off Mr. Smith. When Tiger was close enough to see Mr. Smith, he noticed that Mr. Smith's blue eyes were soft and kind and full of compassion.

As Tiger extended his neck to put his nose in the bucket of oats, Mr. Smith slowly and gently raised his hand to touch Tiger's muzzle. Tiger sniffed Mr. Smith's hand, but was still afraid and backed away. Yet, when Tiger looked at the kind, loving eyes of Mr. Smith, he gathered up the courage to get close to him again. This time, Tiger allowed Mr. Smith to touch his muzzle softly. Mr. Smith's touch was as kind and gentle as his blue eyes, and Tiger was no longer afraid. Tiger dipped his nose in Mr. Smith's bucket of oats and happily ate them all.

From then on, every day when Mr. Smith came to bring Tiger oats and hay, a happy Tiger would run across the green pasture to the fence to meet his friend. Sometimes, remembering his beatings from the past, Tiger would hesitate before approaching the fence. Yet Mr. Smith was always patient and always spoke kindly. Eventually, Tiger would approach Mr. Smith at the fence with no hesitation. Tiger would run to Mr. Smith and allow him to rub his muzzle, pat his back, and feed him delightful oats from his bucket.

PART THREE

Over time, Tiger and Mr. Smith became great friends. One day, Mr. Smith began teaching Tiger good things for mules to know. Tiger learned how to walk right beside Mr. Smith, step by step. When Mr. Smith would stop, Tiger would stop. When Mr. Smith would begin walking, Tiger would begin walking. Tiger also learned the proper way to pass through a gate and how to stand still when Mr. Smith gave the command.

When it was time for grooming, Tiger agreeably allowed Mr. Smith to pick up his feet and trim his hooves. When it was time for work, Tiger learned to put his head down when he needed a halter. Tiger learned some funny tricks, too, like climbing up stairs and jumping over logs. Tiger's most famous trick was standing on a tree stump. A mule standing proudly on a tree stump acting like he is a king is a funny sight to see, but Tiger loved to impress Mr. Smith and his friends with his very best trick.

Occasionally Tiger resisted learning new things. When Tiger would disobey, Mr. Smith would correct Tiger with a gruff voice and a thump between his eyes, because Mr. Smith did not tolerate rude behavior. Then, Tiger remembered to obey Mr. Smith and did as he was told. Tiger wondered why his first owner didn't discipline him with a simple thump instead of beating him.

One day, Mr. Smith began teaching Tiger a more difficult procedure—carrying a pack on his back. The pack was big, heavy, and uncomfortable. Tiger did not like it at all, so he began kicking and bucking to try to get the pack off his back. All the kicking and bucking stirred up dust and made a mess, yet no matter how hard Tiger tried, he couldn't get the pack off his back. Tiger didn't understand what was on his back, which made him feel scared. Mr. Smith simply stood and watched patiently because he knew Tiger was afraid.

Eventually, Tiger became too tired to resist. With his head down in defeat, Tiger sluggishly walked to a nearby fence corner. Mr. Smith slowly approached Tiger and quietly whispered, "Everything is all right, boy. You're my boy. Everything is going to be all right."

Tiger loved to hear Mr. Smith's still, small whispers because they always calmed him down and eased his fears.

Next, Mr. Smith readjusted the pack, re-tightened the straps, and led Tiger around the pasture until Tiger got used to the pack on his back.

Every day for a week, Mr. Smith would put the pack on Tiger's back and walk Tiger around. Next, Mr. Smith started placing sacks of corn in the bags to make them heavier. Though it seemed awkward at first, Tiger got used to carrying the heavy load as long as Mr. Smith was with him.

Most days, Tiger spent his time romping in the big, green pasture. He enjoyed smelling the wild flowers and listening to the songs of the birds, frogs, and insects. On special days, Mr. Smith, atop his Appaloosa mare named Bella, would lead Tiger on trail rides around the farm. Tiger loved spending this time with Bella and Mr. Smith. However, Tiger didn't know that Mr. Smith was strengthening Tiger to take him on a very special trip with Bella to the mountains in the summer.

When summer came, Mr. Smith loaded up Bella and Tiger and drove to Colorado to stay for the entire summer. Tiger thought Colorado was the most beautiful place he had ever seen. He was amazed at the big mountains, cool air, and all the room to play. Tiger was confident and proud as he carried Mr. Smith's camping gear high into the Rocky Mountains. Mr. Smith was delighted when Tiger began getting in front and leading the way along the trails. Mr. Smith had seen Tiger grow from a scared, abused, little mule to a strong, poised leader. Mr. Smith, Tiger, and Bella enjoyed traveling and camping in the majestic mountains all summer long.

When they came back to Tennessee, Mr. Smith had a new lesson to teach Tiger. This time, Mr. Smith put a saddle and bridle on Tiger. This was new to Tiger, so he was a little nervous. Next, Mr. Smith sat atop the saddle Tiger was wearing. Mr. Smith knew Tiger was powerful enough to buck him off the saddle and onto the ground, yet he trusted the mule because Tiger was now his loyal friend. As time went by, Tiger carried Mr. Smith all over the beautiful, green countryside of Tennessee.

Together, Mr. Smith and Tiger still travel up and down steep hills, trot through streams, camp, and play. Tiger still learns new lessons too, like helping Mr. Smith open gates and standing still as Mr. Smith shoots his bow and arrow while sitting on Tiger's strong, sturdy back.

As time goes by, the bond between Mr. Smith and Tiger continues to grow. They both have learned how much can be accomplished with love, kindness, and trust.

WHAT IS A MULE?

A mule is the offspring of a male donkey (jack) and a female horse (mare). Except for their long ears, which come from the donkey side, they look very much like a horse.

Their muscle composition is different from a horse, however. A mule's muscles are longer and smoother than a horse—and although both are very strong, pound for pound a mule is typically stronger and built for endurance.

A mule is also very sure-footed and can traverse through very difficult terrain.

A mule is often referred to as stubborn. In reality, this characteristic is actually self-preservation. A mule will freeze and simply refuse to go anywhere it considers unsafe or uncertain.

Mules are also loving and loyal animals and are actually attracted to humans, another notable trait that is passed down from the donkey.

Treated with patience and kindness, a mule can be a lifelong friend.

THE AUTHOR

J. ALLAN SMITH's experience with troubled teens in public education, his work with rescued mules on the family farm, and his faithfulness to our awesome God has led him to share the road of recovery story of *Tiger the Mule*. He has a story to share that not only speaks to how to treat these hybrid equine, but lessons we all can use to help young people who face difficulties in life.

THE ILLUSTRATOR

Thank you to **D.W. SMITH,** my brother, for his gifted ability to illustrate Tiger and me so realistically.

D.W. Smith, artist and illustrator, can be reached at: wsdaniel83@yahoo.com

FOR EDUCATIONAL PROGRAMMING:

If your school, church, library, bookstore, or business is interested in scheduling a book signing, book reading, or a visit with Tiger the mule and Mr. Smith, you may contact them at bitterootman@yahoo.com.

CPSIA information can be obtained
at www.ICGtesting.com
Printed in the USA
LVHW071111020519
616021LV00002B/5/P